To my three angels; Barb, Heather and MacKenzie.

Barb and Heather; *without your unselfish caring,*
unfailing support and persistent encouragement,
this book would still be in the file folder.

MacKenzie; *your first two weeks on this earth spent*
in the intensive care unit was meant to gather your family
around you and awaken us to the precious and fragile
gift of life. And look at you now! You give us days full of joy,
immeasurable moments of surprise and most of all a
deepening and growing sense of hope. You are truly an angel
sent to us from God. Papaw loves you.

Special thanks to Spin Cycle Marketing Communications, Inc. Cleveland, Ohio for their remarkable creative talent and their overwhelming generosity.

In a place not too far from here

Lives a dog, his friends

And the adventures they share!

He was given the name Sir Sniffsalot,

Because his nose never seems to stop a lot!

And he has long, shaggy hair the color of chocolate.

Now, you should know that Sir Sniffsalot

Gets into trouble more often than not!

His nose just goes and goes and never can stop!

And it bumps into things that it really should not.

He can smell anything, poor Sniffsalot,

And it doesn't even have to smell a lot.

He can smell things that are sweet or have begun to rot.

He can even smell things that you never would thought!

One day he was sniffing while out on a walk

And he sniffed the pies from a pie baker's shop.

He ran through the door and before he could stop

His nose got stuck in the cherry pie pot!

The baker chased Sir Sniffsalot,

But he slipped and crashed into the pans and pots.

And Sir Sniffsalot ran fast down the walks

Banging and bumping into shoes and socks!

With the cherry pie pot still stuck to his nose

Sir Sniffsalot couldn't see where to go!

He fell and he tumbled and bumped his head

And the cherry pie pot flew over a shed!

Sir Sniffsalot ran straight to his house.

He ran inside and startled a mouse!

He was oh so tired from sniffing a lot!

So he curled up to sleep on his cot

Just so his nose could rest a lot!

Sir Sniffsalot has a very best friend

Whose nose just sniffs and sniffs and sniffs with no end!

She is creamy colored with raspberry spots.

A beautiful dog named Dally Polka Dots!

Her ears are long and floppy and furry

And, just like Sir Sniffsalot she has to scurry!

She loves to put her nose to the ground

And smell every smell that there is to be found.

She sniffs at the ant hills, the bushes and trees,

And even the fence posts and the bumble bees.

She sniffs at the spiders that jump on her nose.

She even smells the honey bee inside the rose!

Dally Polka Dots smells things that she shouldn't

And lots of things you and I couldn't!

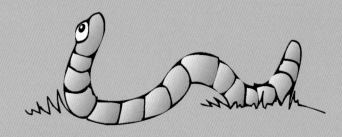

She sniffs giant tree trunks and mail box poles,

Old paper wrappers and craw daddy holes!

She never looks up—her nose just sniffing and blowing.

Crossing this road and that road,

Dally never thinks of where she is going!

She sniffs the beetles and worms and frogs,

The grass hoppers and clover and old rotten logs.

She sniffs the butterflies, lady bugs and fat warty toads,

And she found herself lost after crossing too many roads!

Dally Polka Dots brought her nose up from the ground,

And thought she was lost and would never be found!

Which frog was it? Which beetle was that?

What cricket was it that smelled like that?

She tried to remember what smell was with who,

But there were too many smells and too many who's!

A hundred frogs and a thousand toads,

A million crickets and how many roads?

Ten thousand grass hoppers and maybe more.

Poor Dally was lost, that's for sure!

Wait a minute! What is that smell?

Is that Sir Sniffsalot? She just couldn't tell.

Her nose went up and then it went down.

It went side to side and then all around!

It was Sir Sniffsalot right there beside her!

He had waited for Dally along with a spider!

The spider you see had watched from a tree

As Dally smelled toads,

And crossed all those roads.

He watched as she sniffed her way through the clover

Around and around the same field—over and over!

Poor Dally Polka Dots had smelled her way through it.

She had gone round in circles and never knew it!

Sir Sniffsalot and Little Miss Lollygag

Sir Sniffsalot has another best friend.

And she can't keep up when the others run!

Her name is Little Miss Lollygag

And she has a very, very slow tail wag!

Her fur is thick and oh so long

She can barely walk without falling down!

It hangs down her face and across her snout

And it covers her eyes so she has to peek out!

It's so long in fact that she has no chin,

And you just can't tell where her legs end and begin!

Her bright yellow tail swishes this way and that.

She never goes fast, she just isn't like that.

She goes left and then right, Little Miss Lollygag.

From this side to that with a zig and a zag!

Sir Sniffsalot and all of his friends

Just let her wander 'til the day light ends.

They watch her roll in the grass close by

Making sure to keep a watchful eye!

Her nose goes where her tail should be

And she wanders 'round almost every tree!

She wanders over walkways and driveways,

And you never know when she might walk sideways!

She takes as much time, no matter what.

And rolls on her back with her legs straight up!

Little Miss Lollygag just daydreams and wonders

About everything from sunshine to thunder!

She wonders about the wind and the sky.

And how is it that birds can fly?

She wonders and wanders and falls farther behind.

But, Little Miss Lollygag just doesn't mind.

She wants to see all that there is to see.

Her mind simply running with curiosity!

She doesn't care that her nose isn't racing.

Little Miss Lollygag has dreams that she's chasing!

Sir Sniffsalot has two special friends

Two bunny rabbits—identical twins!

One friend is named Hop and the other Squat

And they do things exactly the same a lot!

Their ears are floppy and exactly alike,

And their fluffy tails look perfectly right!

They hop and squat at the exact same time

And sit in the grass like two of a kind!

Hop and Squat eat carrots for lunch,

The kind that come in a perfect bunch!

They sit together so tight in a crunch,

And match each other munch for munch!

Is there an easy way to tell Squat from Hop?

You cannot tell from their ears as they flop!

Can you tell Hop from Squat just from their tails?

Not as they hop and squat down the trails!

There is one special way to tell Squat from Hop.

They are so very different, our Hop and Squat.

You see, Hop is purple the color of plums

And Squat is bright yellow, just like the sun!

Sir Sniffsalot's nose was running this day

To smells of something very far away.

It took him to a place he had never been

A place so rotten, so fowl and so grim!

The smells were strong with lots of stink.

Like something left in the kitchen sink!

He walked and walked with his nose to the ground

And nothing, oh nothing could turn him around!

He could smell sour milk and rotten eggs,

Mashed potatoes and old chicken legs.

Bologna sandwiches and thrown out pies.

Slimy yogurt and old French fries!

Sir Sniffsalot just couldn't stop

Until he reached the place that smelled a lot.

He ran faster and faster to the big smelly lump,

And found himself right in the middle of the garbage dump!

With so many smells and so much stink.

Sir Sniffsalot's nose didn't know what to think!

He buried his nose and wallowed the while

In every smelly, stinky, disgusting pile.

He learned that the dump was no place for a dog.

'Cause the smells just clung to his hair like smog!

He was in there so long all the smells became one,

And he smelled just like the dump before he was done!

The garbage rot had made his nose sore.

It was so smelly he just couldn't take any more.

He got home late that night smelling like an old sink

So Sir Sniffsalot took a bath to get rid of the stink!